Read-A-Rhyme

Mother Goose's Bedtime Rhymes

Illustrated by Tammie Speer-Lyon

Modern Publishing
A Division of Unisystems, Inc.
New York, New York 10022
Series UPC #19585

Wee Willie Winkie runs through the town,
Upstairs and downstairs, in his nightgown,
Rapping at the window, crying through the lock,
"Are all the children in their beds?
It's now eight o'clock."

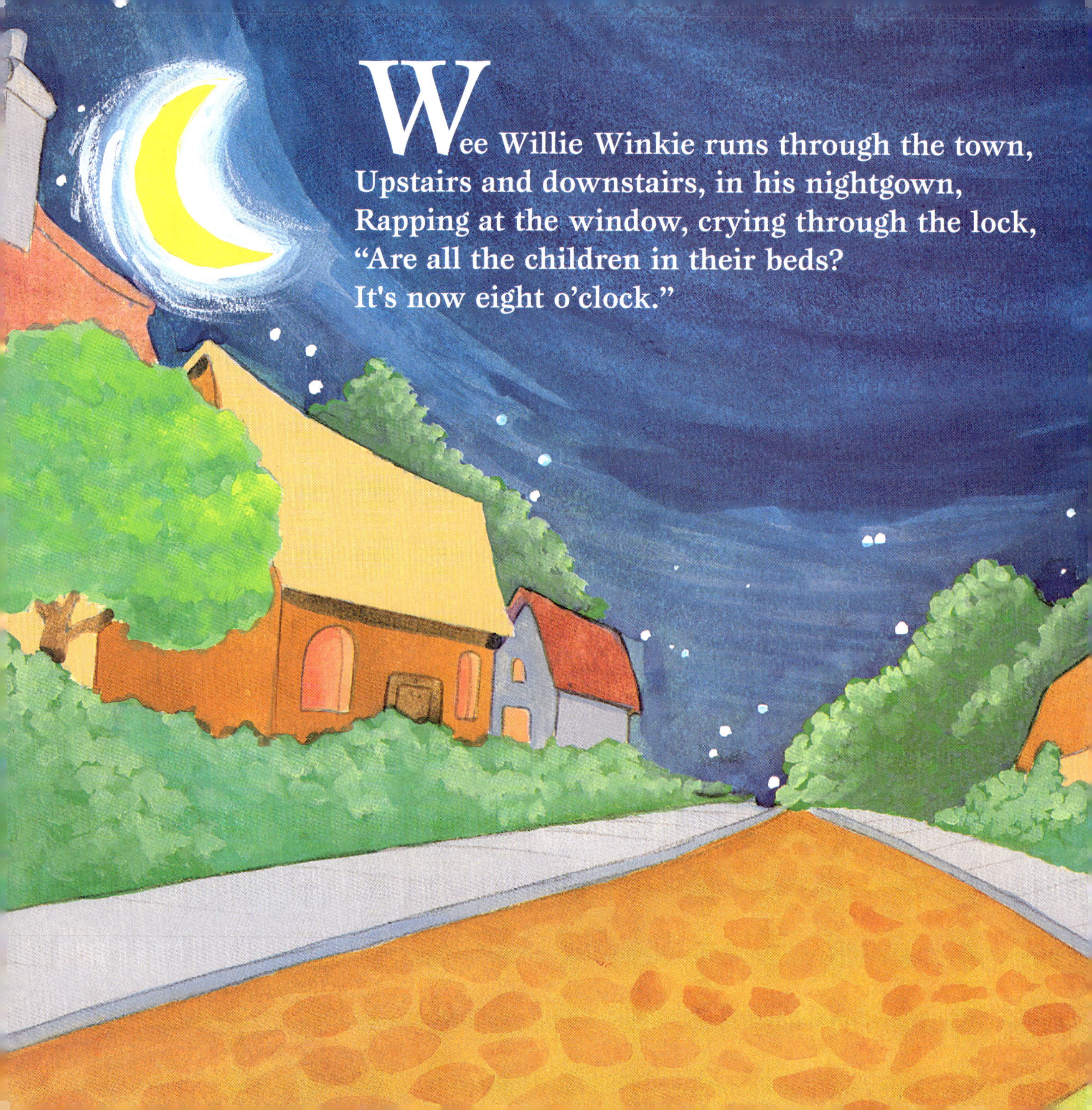

The Man in the Moon looked
out of the moon,
Looked out of the moon and said,
"'Tis time that, now I'm getting up,
All children are in bed."

Twinkle, twinkle, little star,
How I wonder what you are.
Up above the world so high,
Like a diamond in the sky,
Twinkle, twinkle, little star,
How I wonder what you are.

Girls and boys, come out to play!
The moon doth shine as bright as day.
Leave your supper and leave your sleep,
And come with your playfellows into the street.
Come with a whoop, come with a call,
Come with a good will or not at all.
Up the ladder and down the wall,
A half-penny roll will serve us all.
You find milk, and I'll find flour,
And we'll have a pudding in half an hour.

There was an old woman
who lived in a shoe.
She had so many children,
she didn't know what to do.
She gave them some broth,
without any bread;
She beat them all soundly
and sent them to bed.

Bye, baby bunting,
Daddy's gone a-hunting,
To get himself a rabbit skin
To wrap his baby bunting in.

Hush, little baby, don't say a word;
Mama's gonna buy you a mockingbird.

If that mockingbird won't sing,
Mama's gonna buy you a diamond ring.

If that diamond ring turns brass,
Mama's gonna buy you a looking glass.

If that looking glass gets broke,
Mama's gonna buy you a billy goat.

If that billy goat won't pull,
Mama's gonna buy you a cart and bull.

If that cart and bull break down,
You'll still be the sweetest little baby in the town.

Rock-a-bye, baby, on the treetop,
When the wind blows, the cradle will rock.
When the bough breaks, the cradle will fall,
And down will come baby, cradle and all.

Hush-a-bye, baby,
lie still with thy daddy,
Thy mammy has gone to the mill,
To get some meal to bake a cake,
So pray, my dear baby,
lie still.

Sleep, baby, sleep;
Our cottage vale is deep;
The little lamb is on the green,
With woolly fleece so soft and clean;
Sleep, baby, sleep.

Sleep, baby, sleep,
Down where the woodbines creep;
Be always like the lamb so mild,
A kind and sweet and gentle child.
Sleep, baby, sleep.

Up wooden hill,
Down sheet lane,
Cross pillow bank,
And here we are again.

Rock-a-bye, baby, thy cradle is green;
Father's a nobleman, mother's a queen;
And Betty's a lady and wears a gold ring,
And Johnny's a drummer and drums for the king.

Go to bed late,
Stay very small;
Go to bed early,
Grow very tall.

I see the moon,
And the moon sees me.
The moon sees the one
That I want to see.

God bless the moon,
And God bless me.
God bless the one
That I want to see.

Star light, star bright,
First star I see tonight,
I wish I may, I wish I might
Have the wish I wish tonight.

Diddle, diddle, dumpling, my son John
Went to bed with his breeches on,
One shoe off and one shoe on,
Diddle, diddle, dumpling, my son John.

When little Fred went to bed,
He always said his prayers.
He kissed Mama and then Papa,
And straightway went upstairs.

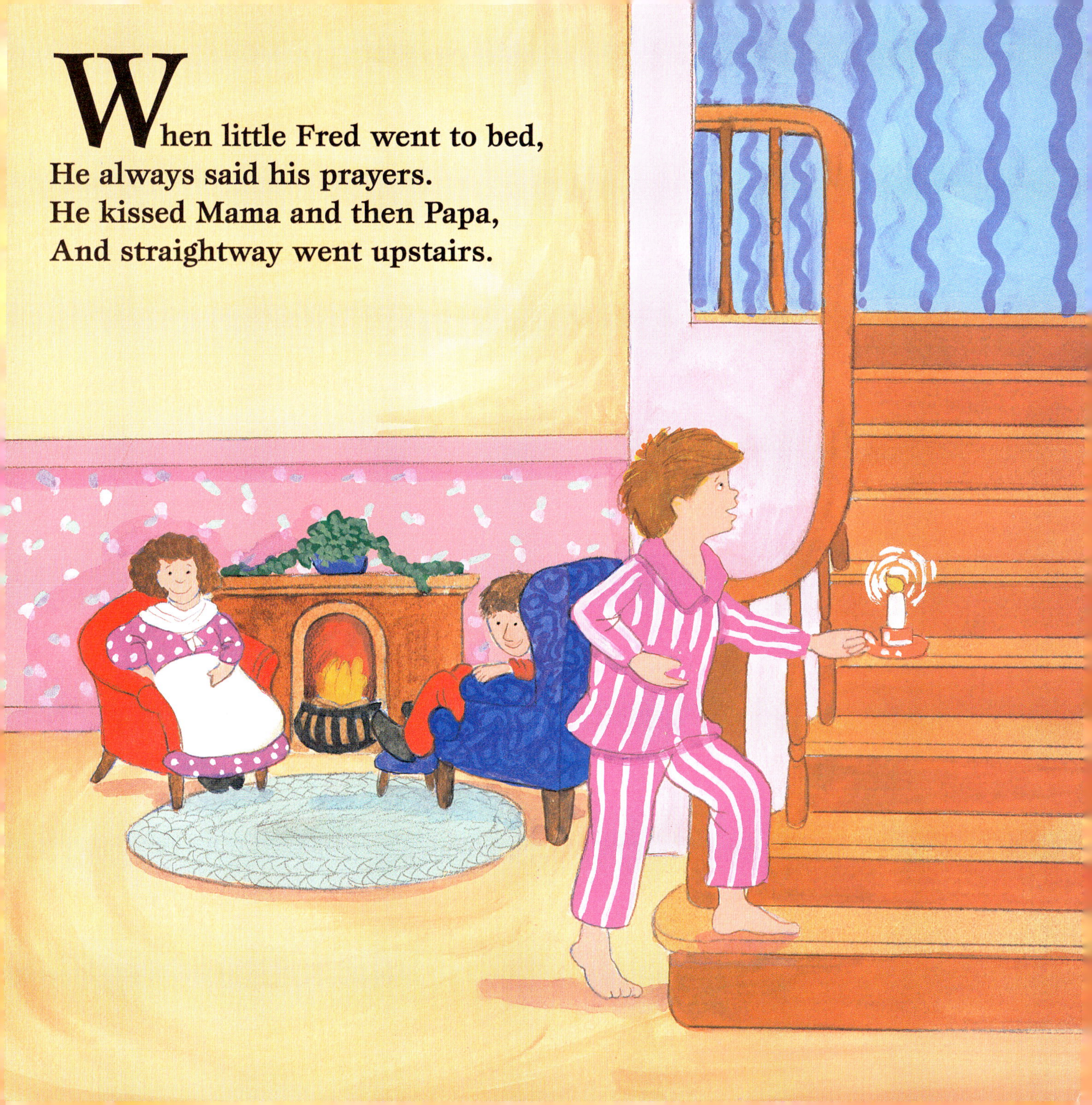

Three jolly gentlemen in coats of red
Rode their horses up to bed.

Three jolly gentlemen snored till morn,
Their horses champing the golden corn.

Three jolly gentlemen, at break of day,
Came clitter-clatter down the stairs
And galloped away.

And now,
good night;
Our play is done;
Farewell to each
And every one.